Samuel French Acting Edition

D1234469

A Life

by Adam Bock

SAMUELFRENCH.COM   SAMUELFRENCH.CO.UK

ISBN 978-0-573-70612-7

www.SamuelFrench.com
www.SamuelFrench.co.uk

FOR PRODUCTION ENQUIRIES

UNITED STATES AND CANADA
Info@SamuelFrench.com
1-866-598-8449

UNITED KINGDOM AND EUROPE
Plays@SamuelFrench.co.uk
020-7255-4302

Each title is subject to availability from Samuel French, depending
upon country of performance. Please be aware that *A LIFE* may not be
licensed by Samuel French in your territory. Professional and amateur
producers should contact the nearest Samuel French office or licensing
partner to verify availability.

MUSIC USE NOTE

IMPORTANT BILLING AND CREDIT REQUIREMENTS

A LIFE had its world premiere at Playwrights Horizons (Tim Sanford, Artistic Director; Leslie Marcus, Managing Director; Carol Fishman, General Manager) in New York on September 30, 2016. The production was directed by Anne Kauffman. The scenic design was by Laura Jellinek, the costume design was by Jessica Pabst, the lighting design was by Matt Frey, and the sound design was by Mikhail Fiksel. The Production Stage Manager was Erin Gioia Albrecht. The cast was as follows:

NATE MARTIN.....................................David Hyde Pierce

CURTIS..Brad Heberlee

ELLEN / ASSISTANT................................Nedra McClyde

MEDICAL EXAMINER / MORTICIAN .... Marinda Anderson

OTHER MEDICAL EXAMINER / NATE'S SISTER... Lynne McCollough

A LIFE was originally commissioned and produced by Portland Center Stage in Portland, Oregon (Chris Coleman, Artistic Director; Rose Riordan, Associate Artistic Director) and was developed, in part, at the 2015 Sundance Institute Writing Studio at Flying Point.

CHARACTERS

NATE MARTIN – fifty-four
CURTIS – mid-forties
ELLEN / ASSISTANT – played by Actress #1
MEDICAL EXAMINER / MORTICIAN – played by Actress #2
OTHER MEDICAL EXAMINER / NATE'S SISTER – played by Actress #3

SETTING

A wall. A door. An Eames sofa. Chairs. Tables. Whatever is needed.
New York City.

TIME

Now.

AUTHOR'S NOTES

Four years ago my parents died. First my mother and then, seven weeks later, my father. He was always a gentleman, and he loved her and she loved him, and I tell people he held the door for her and then followed her through it.

It was sudden and shocking and heartbreaking and incomprehensible. Thrown around by the noisy emotion following their deaths, I remember feeling untethered from the world, wondering how were things possibly continuing as before? Why was nothing changed?

As time went on I realized that I'd changed. Or was changing. Without parents I could no longer be a child. Or when I was childish, I felt odd and slightly fraudulent. At this very late date it was time to grow up.

What does it take to change? Does disaster have to strike a loud, clanging bell before we wake up?

In Quaker meeting Quakers sit quietly. They stop the chatter of the world, hoping to hear the voice of God. I love that they do it together, that they go against the noisy current of the rushing world, that they wait, that they hope.

I love that in the theater we sit together, that we sit in a small room that seems to float somewhere above the hurdy-gurdy of New York, that we listen carefully, and that we hope.

I think we hope to see something that will shock us out of our steady lives, to see something that will encourage us to make the changes we secretly know we need to make. God or no god maybe, or Dionysus, or maybe even some small god we don't know at all singing and encouraging us as the actors play out the possibility of something new.

Dedicated to Susan Cheever, Matt Farnsworth, Jason Butler Harner, and Lucy Thurber. Because they helped me make it through.

1.

NATE *sits on an Eames sofa, the compact one.*
It's a slender, minimalist piece of classic mid-
century furniture. There is an elegant reading
lamp standing near the sofa. Some books. A
couple of astrological charts printed on 8x11
paper. He talks to the audience.

NATE. Mark broke up with me a month ago and I've been searching through my astrology chart and through his chart, trying to figure out what happened.

Isn't it hard that the truth hides itself so well? It sits in some small corner in a dim light, smiling but not saying anything and, if we're lucky, we stumble across it and then we have to use any means at our disposal to flush it out, to make it show itself.

And then once it does, when the truth does show itself, isn't it weird that we move on so quickly, that we accept it, we go: Oh huh, I guess that's true, huh. Huh.

And then

Waving his hand: "We move on."

we move on?

It's weird we don't stop and pat ourselves on the back for figuring that truth out, or stop to really think about it and let it sink in.

Instead, I don't know about you but I rush on.

Sometimes I catch myself when I'm way past that moment of figuring something out, I catch myself and I look back and I think: Wait a minute, did I miss something else back there? Did I rush on too quickly?

Okay. Wait a minute. There was. Something else. Besides the thing I figured out. I think. And I did miss it. I think.

And: I wonder what it was?

And then: Oh no oh no what was the thing I figured out? I've already forgotten it, I think I just forgot it.

I missed something and I forgot something.

A bunch of important things just happened and now they're gone. Great.

Narrowed eyes, thinking.

The truth is so hard to find and it's almost impossible to hold onto.

In the street outside, we hear some guy yell: "Gary! Gary! Gary! Gary! Gary! Gary!"

That's a guy who's always yelling for some Gary guy. The city is noisy. Sometimes I can barely hear myself think.

NATE *looks at his phone. Mark hasn't texted him.*

I didn't always believe in astrology.

When I was in my thirties, I was living in Providence, in Rhode Island, in an apartment on the third floor of an old Victorian.

The building was chock-full of people.

There was a hair salon on the first floor, with a sign out front that said Georges, it was in italics, Georges with an s but there was no apostrophe, which suggested that it was owned by some Georges, some hairdresser, some man from France,

it didn't say George's

Makes an apostrophe gesture.

owned by George,

even though the owner of the hair salon wasn't any Georges from France.

His name wasn't even George! His name was Ray. I think he was from Cranston.

Shrugs.

There was also a dress shop on the first floor, and a bead shop full of all different kinds of beads and it was always full of people who loved beads and making all sorts of different kinds of beaded things.

On the second floor, there was another shop that sold second-hand clothes and more dresses. And a small office where two accountants worked, a mother and her daughter, the Cains, the daughter's name was Candace. Candy. Cain. Yeah. I'm not making this up. Candy Cain.

Thinks.

That must have been hard in high school. You'd have to be a good sport about it. Candy Cain.

And there was another dress shop on the second floor. Isn't that weird? To have so many dress shops in one building? How many dress shops do you need?

I lived on the top floor of the building in a long shotgun apartment. At one end of a long hall there was a kitchen and a bathroom.

Halfway down the hall, there was a living room of sorts and my bedroom.

Down at the other end of the hall there were two more rooms, doors shut, because those rooms were full of crap that generations of my occasional roommates, full of the crap they'd decided they couldn't fit in their cars when they left so they left it and that I left there because I didn't know whether they were going to come back for it.

I had so much space in that apartment. It was so different from New York. If someone leaves something here for more than a day or two if I can't get them on the phone to say "Come and get your stuff," I'm like "That goes out, that goes out on the street," "I'm putting that out on the sidewalk," and I'm ruthless, even if it's a family heirloom or some –

This one roommate I had in Providence left a photography enlarger in one of those backrooms. An enlarger! It was huge. And a box of photographs she'd taken herself, left all that back there, for two years! Can you imagine? Because she moved to Austin. And she couldn't fit them in her car. And she left her cats. Two of them.

Holds up two fingers, eyes wide.

She finally came back to get the cats. And she was "Where's my enlarger?" and I was "I gave it away." And she was mad.

So anyway, one day when I was living in Providence, one day all of a sudden I lost faith in everything I'd ever learned. Just like that.

Up until that moment I'd used books, and thinking, to try and figure things out.

Shakes his head.

The woman who ran the second-hand clothes store on the second floor was named Daniela and we were pals. And that day, when I'd lost faith in everything I'd ever learned, I went and told her and she said "Oh my gosh. Oh my gosh. Oh my gosh." Yeah. Yeah.

But then she was "You could start over and you could study astrology and that might," because she was a firm believer. In it. And all sorts of other things like tarot and crystals and. But mostly astrology.

I was like "I don't know Daniela." But she said "Just let me do your chart. Can't hurt, right?" So I was like "Okay," and she did and then she looked at it and said "Oh my gosh, oh my gosh, in two weeks you're going to get a whole lot of money and you're going to meet someone golden." Because Jupiter was doing something funny, trining my sun or something, something, in my eighth house or and of course I was "Okay!" But I was skeptical because I was broke and I couldn't see any money coming, not from anywhere.

But then two weeks later I got approved for my very first credit card and my parents gave me a car! Yeah. Yeah. Because my sister was getting married and they were helping pay for the wedding and they knew I wasn't ever going to get married so that wasn't fair, cash-wise, so they gave me their old car. As a sort of "We won't talk about it, but here is a consolation prize because you're not going to get married, are you."

A car! That was exciting. I had to learn how to drive. Because my dad was the designated driving instructor in my family and we didn't see eye-to-eye when I was sixteen.

So before I could go home to pick up the car, my friend Rebecca had to teach me how to drive. She borrowed her sister's new car to do it, stupid, but sweet, but stupid, new car and me. She took me out, first to the parking lot of the Wild Oats and then out on the highway and I knew I was getting better at driving when she would only put one foot up on the dashboard. Instead of both feet and sometimes her hands. Like.

> *Hands braced against an imaginary dashboard.*

I never told her, whenever I had to drive through a tight spot, I'd shut my eyes and just push the gas petal down hard and hope for the best.

I should call Rebecca. I haven't talked to her in so long. Gimme a second.

> *He calls her. Doesn't get her, so hangs up.*

(Mutters:) I'm just going to write that down on my to-do list.

> *He writes it down.*

I got so lucky when I went in for my driver's license. I was waiting in line for the driving portion of the test. In front of me was this little old Vietnamese lady, she had to be sixty or seventy, and I figured "If she can do it, I can do it."

Then I took the written part of the test. Jesus. Some of those questions? How far from the curb, how fast when you're so many feet behind, stuff like that?

When I took my answers up to the desk to find out how I did, the lady corrected it and went "Oh darn, you got only seventeen out of twenty right and you needed to get eighteen." And I was "Oh darn." And she was like "Yeah." And she looked at me

Tilts his head.

And I looked at her.

Tilts his head. Smiles. A little sad.

But then she said "If you hadn't put E on number three, what would you have put instead?" And I said "I dunno. What would you have put?" And she said "I would have put B." So I said "Well, then I guess I would put B, too." And she said "Okay then, let's just put B for number three." And she passed me!

Oh and the same week my parents gave me the car I met Yan. Who was German and a Leo. The lion. He had gold hair. "You're going to get a lot of money and you're going to meet someone golden." I got a credit card, I got a car and I got Yan! So. I was –

Eyes open.

I love astrology.

It's a science. It's a science that uses charts and mathematics to try to figure out how the sun and the moon and the planets, all of them, Mercury and Venus and Mars and Jupiter, Saturn, Uranus, and Neptune and Pluto, even though some people think Pluto isn't a planet anymore, it's a science that tries to figure out how the planets and the constellations and where they all were in the sky when you were born, how all that is influencing your personality, and therefore your future.

This is my chart.

It's a like a snapshot of the heavens the moment I was born.

It's as if when I opened my eyes up to the sky for the very first time, all of this imprinted on me.

Looks up.

It's very enticing, really. The idea of looking at this and having some idea of how all this –

Waves vaguely at himself and at the whole world around him.

how all this works.

I mean you can look at your chart and see things and go "Huh. Maybe that's why I –"

Your chart is like a big pie, divided into twelve slices. See? And each of these little pie slices in the circle is called a "house" and each pie slice "house" rules or explains a different part of your life. And you can look at that little slice and see what sign rules it and which planets were in it when you were born and which other planets are sending it energy and you can understand stuff.

For example the first house, here, this pie slice is called the house of self. Any planets that are in your first house are really important. Pluto is in my first house. Pluto, god of the underworld and death. That was a little worrying. I was like "Daniela?" But she said "Oh no, that's good." I was like "Really?" and she was like "Yeah, because Pluto also represents transformation, the ability to change." So supposedly I can change.

That top line of the first house pie slice is called your rising sign. My rising sign is in Virgo. Your rising sign is the first impression you give others, how you present yourself to the world. So, for example, even though my sun is in Scorpio, people see me and think I'm a Virgo. Daniela said "If people tell you you're kind of picky, don't worry about it, it's just because you're a Virgo rising. And it just means you like details. And not everybody does. But that's not your fault. So."

The second house is called the money house because it shows you what kind of relationship you'll have with money in your life, what kind of resources, what kind of stuff you'll have, right at hand. Some people have Jupiter in their second house and because Jupiter rules luck, they're totally lucky with money, it comes flying at them. It just shows up everywhere and they never have to worry about running out of cash.

The third house tells you whether you'll be any good at communicating. My sun is in my third house. Daniela said that's why I like to talk so much.

And as you spin through the rest of the houses, you can figure out what kind of home would be comfortable for you, how you could have fun and play, what'll keep you healthy, what kinds of friends you might have and about sex and school and your career and your group affiliations and finally what secrets will allow you to grow.

I think my grandmother's second house, her money house, I think it must have been lit up like a Christmas tree. I bet she had loads of planets stuffed in there. She liked things way more than she liked people. But really, she did.

She'd look at a chair with more fondness than her daughter, my mother. The chair was more constant maybe, or had more character than my mom, who was always trying to please her. That was a hopeless task. Mom should have just said "Forget it!" and left my grandmother to her stuff-filled apartment and her vodka. But you know how it is, you want to please that person who refuses to smile back at you, especially if it's your mother.

> *Looks at his phone. Mark hasn't texted him.*
> *Puts his phone down. Then it rings.*

Oh sorry. That's Curtis. I'm just –

> *Answers.*

Hey. I can't talk. Can I call you later? Okay.

> *Hangs up.*

That was my friend Curtis. He's my best friend. People are always asking me "Why don't you date him?" I'm like "I'm not going to date Curtis. He's my best friend."

Or they're like "I got a guy for you. I work with him. I know you'd like each other because you both like eating." Or something like that.

I asked Daniela if my chart could tell me who I should go out with and she was like "Sure!" But before I could find out more, our landlord jacked up her rent and she had to move her store over to Pawtucket and I didn't see her as much.

But here, see how these two planets are angled like the corners of a square? This other astrologer I talked to told me that means there'll always be a tension between those two energies in my life. Jupiter and Venus battling. Luck and love. Fighting. Daniela hadn't mentioned that.

My first boyfriend's name was Sean. My second boyfriend's name was John. Then I dated a Ron, a Don, a Johan. Then I met another John.

> *Shakes his head: "What the hell?"*

Then I met a Rick. I didn't really like him though. Something didn't feel right.

Dwight and I broke up because one day I said "It wouldn't hurt to get a haircut."

Darryl was from Columbus, Ohio.

I broke up with Peter because he was too nice and bought me too many gifts.

> *Shakes his head.*

Then I had my crisis of faith and then I met Yan.

(Mutters:) Sean John Ron Don Johan John. Yan.

Yan was a golden boy. I really loved him. We were together for a long time.

> *Thinks about Yan. Disappears into himself*
> *for a moment.*

After Yan I met Alfredo in the street and brought him home but by then I'd moved to New York and I had this very little apartment and a loft bed and it turns out it's hard to get a trick up into a loft bed. Right?

When I moved to another apartment, I met Stuart. His teeth were too long. Plus he was mean.

Then I dated Stephen and then I dated Bill. And then Stephen and Bill ended up dating each other. They're still together.

And those are just some of them.

He checks his phone. Puts it away.

Mark's too tall.

I'm in group therapy. Because even though I have astrology, I still don't understand everything. And astrology might be full of shit.

Looks up at the sky.

I mean, come on. If I'm really honest with myself.

Plus my Grandpa Oswald always used to say "Don't put all your eggs in one basket."

I mean, I love astrology, and I am pretty sure I believe it, but I've tried all sorts of things to try and figure all this –

Waves at the world.

out.

I've even gone to church. And to Quaker meeting. That's what Quakers call their church but really it's a bunch of Quaker people who get there and sit down and then they all sit there, in complete silence, and wait, and wait, until someone is moved to stand up and say something from their heart. And then when that person is finished, he or she sits down and everyone waits to see if someone else is going to stand up. And sometimes no one does and then it's over and they stand up and go home.

It's really beautiful. But quiet. But beautiful. The room was cool and clean and the light from the sun was just bright enough to see tiny motes of dust floating in the air. You know how they do that?

Floats his hands.

And I went to a meditation class with my friend Jessica. But that was with a bunch of Buddhist monks and we all walked in a circle, not talking, and I got so dizzy from not talking that I had to go sit in the stairwell and put my head down between my knees.

Group is noisier. Which is thank god because I'm not always great with quiet.

Group is me and two therapists and ten other gay guys in a circle for an hour and a half on Thursday nights trying to learn how to tell the truth. It's totally hard because sometimes I'm not even sure what the truth is. But I know I need to be there because my friend Lucy is always teasing me, saying "Oh I just love you!" and then backing the truck up really fast, saying "I'm not going to say anything else! Don't worry about it!" because she can see I'm starting to panic.

I get nervous when it comes to love. I want it but every time I get it I'm afraid I'm going to disappear.

The guys in my group are great.

Sometimes they hold your feet to the fire. One time I was complaining about this weirdo who kept calling me, asking me on dates even though I was already dating Mark and the guys in group got fed up and I remember they were "Just tell him to get lost." And I was "He won't leave me alone!" And they were "He won't leave you alone because you lie to him."

I remember being very offended. I don't lie.

"Oh yes you do!" they said. "You say things like "I don't know right now, I need time, I'm –" or. You lie. You don't tell them "I think you're a freak and I don't want to go out with you." You're a liar. And you don't tell the ones you do like that you like them. You lie to them too. How are they supposed to know you like them?"

Eyes wide open.

One of the guys showed me this diagram.

Shows a diagram to the audience; it's a triangle with "companionship," "passion," and "intimacy" at the three points.

Passion, companionship, intimacy. Passion is sex, companionship is hanging around with each other, and intimacy is being vulnerable and telling the truth. He said that a complete and satisfying love with someone would have all three of these. He said that a one-night stand might only have passion. A love affair might have passion and intimacy but the fact that one of you is betraying a partner might not allow for companionship. Some marriages lose their passion but you might still have intimacy and companionship and that might be enough. But he said you're supposed to aim for all three.

This seems like a lot to hope for.

Shakes head.

"It's not," another guy said and "It's not like you haven't met the right person. You keep meeting him. You just have a fear of intimacy."

I was –

It –

Hm.

Looks at one of his books.

It feels like everyone around me knows what they're supposed to do. Or how the world works or how it's supposed to work and they –

Everybody, all the guys in my group, Curtis, Lucy, it seems like they. As if the world makes sense to them. And I think "Maybe I'm just not listening hard enough or," but –

And here I am looking for love and then when I find it, throwing myself at it and it's it's –

Again.

But when a man falls in love with another man, there is only one thing to do, isn't there? That is: fall, crash through the paper door, tumble down in a rush of arms and legs, to kiss and kiss. To open your heart and say "Come on in, let's see what happens, let's –"

To keep trying?

I tried with Mark. I liked Mark. And I told Mark I liked him.

He wanted me to move in with him. He showed me a closet in his apartment that he'd cleared out for my stuff. It was a small closet but –

And even though there were loads of things in his chart that told me "This might not be the one to," I still said "Yeah yeah. Lemme think about it I'm gonna think about it. Yeah lemme –"

But this year we had so many messy breakups. Me yelling at him or him sitting so silent and dark and not talking to me. We'd fight and then break up and then not talk to each other but then one of us would call and apologize and the other one would apologize too and then there'd be this short delicious honeymoon period when we wanted to listen to each other and smiled at each other. But then we'd fight again and break up but then apologize and listen, fight, break up, apologize, listen, Fight, break up. Apologize, listen. Again. And again.

But then a month ago he made me give him back his New York Rangers jersey.

And then he broke up with me.

And I didn't care at first. I was "Good. Fine. Done."

"See if I care."

    Silence.

"Good."

He keeps not calling me.

I was surprised when all these feelings started to –

I sit and stare at my phone.

Who hasn't waited by the phone? Only to be disappointed when it rings, "Oh it's only Curtis again, calling to see if I'm okay."

He keeps not calling me. He hasn't texted me. He hasn't emailed me.

Then:

I am suddenly crying, or not crying really, trying not to cry but the tears wouldn't stop, so I'm crying, really, and my eyes hurt as I try to squeeze them tight enough to stop the tears, and my stomach hurts.

I don't care. I don't care.

Again.

A long silence.

See these planets? Each of them stands in for a god of something, the god of war, the god of rules, the god of money, of thought, of music, the goddamn goddess of love, and –

And each one of them is a jealous god, unhappy if he is ignored. So spend too much time with one of them, spend all your time dancing with Apollo or hide in the back of the bar talking politics with Mercury –

Be like me and let Venus, let the goddess of love trap you in her glittering net –

And the other gods will come looking for you, and demand that you start paying attention to them instead.

In this life, in the time I have been spending here this time, during this long long visit to this lonely place, Venus has trapped me in her embrace and she refuses to let me go. I breathe and wanting love makes my lungs hurt. When I am alone and think "Oh maybe I've escaped," I look behind me and Venus' little son Eros stands there quietly beckoning to me, telling me his mother wants me to come and worship at her altar again. I walk and he shadows me, skipping along the walls, faint in the bright light of day but always there. Even sleep is no refuge.

And now old, and now single again, a stupid proofreader at a stupid ad agency, now worn out and lonely and uncertain, I don't know how to get away from her.

> *Looks out at the audience. And then away.*

There has to be another way.

I'm going to find someone who knows another way to do all this. I can't live like this anymore.

It's –

It's –

> *Shakes his head.*

> *Laughs. A little too hard. Looks up at the ceiling.*

2.

NATE *and his friend* CURTIS *are in Central Park.*

CURTIS. That's stupid.

NATE. Curtis. Shut up.

CURTIS. Well it is.

NATE. Look at him.

So are we still on for next weekend?

CURTIS. I dunno. My whole family's fighting. Because of my stupid cousin Elena.

NATE. Yeah, so what's new?

CURTIS. So everyone says they don't want to go to Aunt Jane's May Day party.

NATE. But we're still going right? Look at that guy.

CURTIS. I don't know.

NATE. What?

CURTIS. I think I'm going to skip it.

NATE. You're not skipping it. You promised to take me this year.

CURTIS. Everyone'll be fighting.

NATE. I've been dying to go out to your Aunt Jane's for years! And your family's always fighting! That never stopped you from going before. I want to get out of the city.

CURTIS. Look at that guy.

NATE. Look at his arms.

CURTIS. Yum.

NATE. Look at his arms!

CURTIS. Have we seen him before? I feel like I've –

NATE. No. He's new. He's cute.

CURTIS. Lord.

NATE. We should start jogging.

CURTIS. We should.

NATE. We definitely should. We should buy jogging shoes and sweatshirts and jog. Except –

CURTIS. I know.

NATE. Except I hate the jogging part.

CURTIS. Yeah. No.

NATE. It just goes on and on and on.

CURTIS. Be fun if you could just jog a little. Like from here to there.

NATE. And be done with it.

CURTIS. Right?

NATE. Yeah.

CURTIS. He was cute though.

NATE. He was totally cute.

CURTIS. Handsome.

NATE. Be fun to jog behind him.

CURTIS. Right?

NATE. I wish I had arms like those. I'm going to go back to the gym.

CURTIS. Really?

NATE. Shut up.

CURTIS. Remember when that trainer Randy made you buy that juicer? Remember how you drank so much carrot juice your hands turned orange?

NATE. Remember that time I held them up and went "Stop!" and that bicycle messenger thought my hands were a traffic light and he stopped and almost flipped over his handlebars?

CURTIS. "Stop!"

NATE. "Stop!"

CURTIS. Remember how mad that bike messenger was?

NATE. Yeah. Remember how cute Randy was?

CURTIS. He sounded a little intense.

NATE. He was very determined to get me into shape.

CURTIS. I remember you not liking that.

NATE. I liked going to the gym. I liked wearing workout clothes. I liked saying hi to the guys at the front desk. I liked looking at Randy. I can still remember the combination for my lock. Twenty-nine. One. Sixteen.

CURTIS. And you liked the steam room.

NATE. I did. It was very democratic. I remember thinking "This is nice. Everyone gets along in here."
I just didn't like the whole "working out" part. I want to go to your aunt's party, Curtis.

CURTIS. My cousin Elena makes me crazy. She's always. She thinks the world revolves around her and she steals things!

NATE. I never liked her.

CURTIS. That's why there are wars. Because people take things that aren't theirs.

NATE. I really want to go to the party.

CURTIS. It's because she's thirty-six. She's thirty-six and she's not married and so she has to steal my grandfather's watch. I'm not married. I don't go around stealing things.

NATE. You should confront her.

CURTIS. What?

NATE. Yeah! At the party. In front of everyone. Make her give the watch back.

CURTIS. That's a terrible idea.

NATE. I'll stand right next to you when you do it.

CURTIS. My Aunt Jane would kill me. She likes her parties nice.

NATE. You could confront her in the driveway.

CURTIS. What?

NATE. Yeah.

CURTIS. And then jump in the rental car and drive away?

NATE. Yeah. Before your Aunt Jane can yell at you.

CURTIS. I dunno. Look look look. There he is again.

NATE. Look at his arms. Jesus fuck.

CURTIS. Did you call Mark yet?

NATE. No.

CURTIS. Oh.

NATE. No.

CURTIS. I think you should call him, Nate. It's been a while since you had your fight. It's time for you guys to make up.

NATE. It's only been a couple of weeks.

CURTIS. Hasn't it been a month? The longer you leave it, the harder it's going to be.

NATE. He should call me.

CURTIS. Don't you miss him?

NATE. No.

CURTIS. Call him.

NATE. He was the one who broke up with me.

CURTIS. Nate.

NATE. He should call me.

CURTIS. I don't like it when my friends fight. Everyone all around me is fighting and it's exhausting. Oh, Yoga.

> **CURTIS** *nudges* **NATE** *and points out a guy doing yoga on the grass. They watch.*

NATE. Can I ask you something?

CURTIS. Sure.

NATE. And I want you to tell me the truth.

CURTIS. Okay.

NATE. Do you think I have a problem with intimacy?

CURTIS. What?

NATE. The guys in my group seem to think I have a problem with intimacy. I don't even know what they're talking about.

CURTIS. Do you think you have a problem with it?

NATE. I don't know. Maybe?

> **CURTIS** *looks at* **NATE** *carefully.*

NATE. They said that in group the other night and I was going to call you but you were mad at me and I was going to call Allan, but Allan is Allan's not always that helpful.

CURTIS. What do you mean I was mad at you?

NATE. You were.

CURTIS. I wasn't mad at you.

NATE. Because I said that thing about your job.

CURTIS. I didn't care about that.

NATE. Okay.

CURTIS. I didn't.

NATE. Okay but anyway I thought you did and I thought you were mad and I didn't have anyone else to talk to, because most of the other people I know, I don't even know if I should talk to them, I mean I can talk to Lucy or you or sometimes Allan, but you were mad at me and Lucy was in LA.

CURTIS. I wasn't mad at you.

NATE. Anyway, the other night I didn't have you guys to call and I thought "I don't want to call Linda or Jackie or –" and I was like "Isn't it weird I don't want to call my friends?"

Not you and Lucy but –

I was thinking "Isn't it weird? I mean I'm the one who chooses my friends, I chose them right, I mean, Linda and Jackie and Roland? For example? And I don't want to call them?"

And I thought "I have a lot of people around me who talk about themselves a lot. And don't listen. I call them and they start talking and they don't ask anything about me." And I thought "I must like it, listening to them all the time, maybe I find it entertaining?" but then I thought "Maybe it's because if they talk all the time I don't have to share anything that's going on with me."

CURTIS. Huh.

NATE. Half the time, after I get off the phone with them I end up feeling a little crazy.

CURTIS. You're not crazy.

NATE. I dunno.

CURTIS. You're not crazy, Nate.

NATE. I do crazy things though. I talk to people I don't want to talk to. I say yes when I want to say no. I let people yell at me. I don't know how to be honest. I'm always smiling too much. I don't know what I want, I'm too busy trying to figure out what they want instead.

CURTIS. Everyone does those things. Sometimes.

NATE. Anyway so I was "I wish Curtis wasn't mad at me. So I could call him and see if he thinks I have intimacy issues."

CURTIS. You should call Mark. He's who you should talk to. If you want to learn more about being intimate.

NATE. Is your cousin Kevin still going to the party?

CURTIS. Nate.

NATE. I like Kevin.

CURTIS. Kevin's not going to be your boyfriend.

NATE. He –

CURTIS. He's not.

NATE. He's always nice to me.

CURTIS. He's a librarian. He's nice to everyone. Call Mark.

NATE. Kevin's handsome.

CURTIS. He has a girlfriend.

NATE. Oh. Still?

CURTIS. Yes. Call Mark.

3.

NATE's *apartment.* NATE *enters off the street, carrying groceries, mail, and his dry-cleaning. He dumps everything and takes off his shoes and puts on slippers. Hangs up his jacket. Rubs his left arm. Picks up his mail, puts it on his desk. Takes his keys, phone, and wallet out of his pockets and puts them on his desk. Opens and turns on his computer. Picks up his dry-cleaning and puts it in his bedroom. Picks up the groceries and puts them away in his kitchen. Returns to his desk. Opens his mail. Looks at his email. Goes into his kitchen, gets a glass of water.*

A voiceover of his thoughts as he moves around his apartment.

NATE VOICEOVER. Okay let's –

That lady at the – She thinks I'm –

Just don't think about it. Doesn't matter what she thinks. Doesn't even –

This closet is so frigging –

Goddamned Curtis.

He thinks he knows everything. Thinks he knows everything. Thinks. Thinks he knows. Thinks. He.

"Call Mark." Yeah like I'm just going to –

"Call Mark." Mark. Mark. Mark. Mark. I don't –

I've got to vacuum this place.

And put those away.

I gotta get –

I'm –

Did I get the –

NATE *hums. A few verses of a song.*

I'm going to tell them that I don't want to sit next to Michelle anymore at work. I can't take the gum chewing anymore.

Where are my scissors?

Where where –

Ow.

>*He dies of a heart attack, ends up on the floor.*
>
>*Blackout.*

4.

At lights up, **NATE***'s body is still on the floor.*

Then:

In the street outside **NATE***'s building, the sound of a car driving by. The sound of metal cellar doors being opened. A truck stopping, and then the beep of the truck backing up. A honk in the distance. Another car drives by. A long honk.*

Another car drives by. A short warning honk. Another honk. A honk-honk. The quick screech of a tire. A snort and a rumble as a truck drives by.

NATE*'s cell phone rings in his pocket.*

The thrum of **NATE***'s refrigerator turning on.*

Passing in the stairwell outside **NATE***'s door, voices murmur in Albanian, and then the sound of steps.*

We hear the murmur of a television in another apartment.

And the cluck-cluck of pigeons. And a honk. The metal cellar doors are dropped shut. A bus pulls up and idles.

Outside: "Gary! Gary! Gary! Gary! Gary! Gary!"

Another truck rumbles by.

Another honk.

Blackout.

5.

*At lights up, **NATE***'s body is still on the floor.*
His cell phone rings in his pocket.
Blackout.

6.

Lights come up.

The sound of **NATE***'s apartment doorbell.*

CURTIS. *(Offstage.)* The doorbell isn't broken. I can hear it.
Nate?

ELLEN. *(Offstage.)* Mr. Martin?

> *The sound of a key. The apartment building's
> manager,* **ELLEN,** *and* **CURTIS** *enter.*

ELLEN. Mr. Martin?

CURTIS. Nate? Buddy?

> *They see* **NATE***'s body.*

ELLEN. Oh!

> *She starts to high-speed mutter the Hail Mary.*

Hail Mary, full of grace, the Lord is with thee; blessed
are thou among women, and blessed is the fruit of thy
womb, Jesus. Holy Mary. Mother of God, pray for us
sinners, now and at the hour of our death. Amen.

CURTIS. Fuck! Nate! Fuck! Fuck!

> **CURTIS** *rushes over to* **NATE***'s body and feels
> for a pulse.*

Oh fuck. Oh fuck. Oh no.

ELLEN. Is he?

CURTIS. No he's There's no –

ELLEN. Is he breathing?

CURTIS. He's There's no –

ELLEN. Oh. Oh no. Is he?

CURTIS. He's dead he's he's –

ELLEN. Oh no.

> *She exits. Comes back in.*

Oh my god. Oh my god. Oh no.

CURTIS. I couldn't get him on the phone. I tried a bunch of times. And I tried so many times yesterday. I couldn't get him on the phone!

ELLEN. I'm going to call the police.

CURTIS. Yeah. Okay. Okay.

> **ELLEN** *leaves the apartment again.* **CURTIS** *sits on the couch. And cries.*

CURTIS. Darn.

DEAD NATE'S VOICEOVER. What Is that a Is What is that?

CURTIS. Darn.

DEAD NATE'S VOICEOVER. And that? What is that? What –

> **CURTIS** *stands next to* **NATE***'s body.*

I can hear a round sound a low steady something Thump and thump A small Is it a bouncing ball?
And is A wash of water? Or is it is it Maybe it's sand being swept across a floor? I I –

> **CURTIS** *neatens the apartment.*

It's I and hard being in a hallway between here and there. There's never enough light. The –

> *The sounds of a fight in the street. A* **YOUNG WOMAN** *is yelling at her boyfriend.*

YOUNG WOMAN'S VOICE. Because you're an asshole!

YOUNG WOMAN'S FRIEND'S VOICE. Don't touch her!

YOUNG WOMAN'S VOICE. Don't touch me!

YOUNG WOMAN'S FRIEND'S VOICE. Get your hands get your hands –

YOUNG WOMAN'S VOICE. Let go of me!

YOUNG WOMAN'S FRIEND'S VOICE. Get your hands –

BOYFRIEND'S VOICE. I just wanna –

YOUNG WOMAN'S VOICE. I don't care!

YOUNG WOMAN'S FRIEND'S VOICE. She doesn't care!

YOUNG WOMAN'S VOICE. I don't care!

BOYFRIEND'S VOICE. Baby baby come on –

YOUNG WOMAN'S FRIEND'S VOICE. Don't "baby baby" her!

BOYFRIEND'S VOICE. Shut up!

YOUNG WOMAN'S FRIEND'S VOICE. And don't tell me to shut up!

BOYFRIEND'S VOICE. I'll tell you to shut up if you don't stop yapping!

YOUNG WOMAN'S FRIEND'S VOICE. He can't say that to –

YOUNG WOMAN'S VOICE. Don't –

BOYFRIEND'S VOICE. Shut up!

YOUNG WOMAN'S FRIEND'S VOICE. He –

BOYFRIEND'S VOICE. Shut up!

YOUNG WOMAN'S FRIEND'S VOICE. You –

BOYFRIEND'S VOICE. Shut up!

YOUNG WOMAN'S VOICE. Stop –

BOYFRIEND'S VOICE. Shut up!

YOUNG WOMAN'S FRIEND'S VOICE. Oh my GOD!

BOYFRIEND'S VOICE. Both of you! Shut up!

> *Silence. The fight has moved down the street. We hear their muffled voices in the distance. The regular sounds of cars and trucks. And an ambulance in the distance, but driving away from, not toward, the apartment building.*

> **CURTIS** *sits at Nate's desk.*

DEAD NATE VOICEOVER. That's That noise is Curtis.

I can hear him breathing. That's breathing. And that's his heart beating. And that tap tap tap is his shoelace tapping against his shoe. He must be jiggling his foot. He always does that. Okay. Okay.

> **CURTIS** *moves something on Nate's desk.*

Oh. No. I can –

They're going to go through my stuff and throw away things that I love.

7.

A **MEDICAL EXAMINER** *is taking information from* **CURTIS**. **NATE**'s *body is on a gurney.* **ANOTHER MEDICAL EXAMINER** *is zipping it into a body bag and strapping it into the gurney.*

CURTIS. I'm a friend of his.

The **MEDICAL EXAMINER**'s *cellphone rings.*

MEDICAL EXAMINER. Oh sorry just gimme a –

Answers phone.

Hey.

Just wrapping something up here. What are you doing?

Oh. Oh. Wow. Really. How does it drive?

Oh shoot. I lost track of time. No. I can't because I've got another –

Sorry.

Laughs.

Oh sure.

Okay. Okay. See you soon.

Hangs up.

That was my friend Leslie. She bought a Fiat 500L.

OTHER MEDICAL EXAMINER. Does it have those seat warmers?

MEDICAL EXAMINER. I don't know. I didn't ask her. Does he have family in the city?

CURTIS. What?

MEDICAL EXAMINER. Does your friend have family in the city?

CURTIS. No.

MEDICAL EXAMINER. None?

CURTIS. He has a sister in Milwaukee. There isn't anyone else. I'll call her.

MEDICAL EXAMINER. Do you have her number? Our office needs to call her.

CURTIS. You don't want me to –

MEDICAL EXAMINER. You can call her too. We just need to. Legally.

CURTIS. Oh okay. Just –

> **CURTIS** *takes out his phone. Scrolls though it and finds Nate's sister's number.*

Her namc is name is Lori Martin and her number is um four one four – seven three two –

MEDICAL EXAMINER. Four one four – seven two three –

CURTIS. No. Seven three two. Four one four – seven three two –

MEDICAL EXAMINER. Four one four – seven two three –

OTHER MEDICAL EXAMINER. Seven three two. Seven three two.

CURTIS. Seven three two um here look.

> *Shows the number to the first* **MEDICAL EXAMINER.**

MEDICAL EXAMINER. Oh. Seven three two. Okay. Right. Okay.

> *Mumbles the rest of the number. Mumbles "Lori Martin" and "sister."*

Will you be making the arrangements?

CURTIS. Probably.

MEDICAL EXAMINER. Here's my card, my name is Jocelyn Williams. In the future, if you have any questions, this is my number. This is the number of the morgue. These are our hours. If you can't call between these hours, you can leave me a message or a message on the morgue's voicemail.

CURTIS. Okay.

MEDICAL EXAMINER. *(Gives him a form.)* Since you aren't the NoK, his sister will have to sign this and fax or FedEx or email it back to you. It'll designate you as the AI in this case and you'll be able to work with a funeral director.

CURTIS. Do you know a good –

MEDICAL EXAMINER. Let me stop you. We can't recommend or refer you to a specific home. Legally.

OTHER MEDICAL EXAMINER. But there's a good one over on forty-third. Between ninth and tenth.

> **MEDICAL EXAMINER** *looks at* **OTHER MEDICAL EXAMINER.**

MEDICAL EXAMINER. Legally we. Didn't say that.

> *Gives* **CURTIS** *an information sheet.*

On the Federal Trade Commission's website, this is the url, there's a helpful pamphlet called Funerals: a Consumer Guide.

OTHER MEDICAL EXAMINER. Supposedly helpful.

MEDICAL EXAMINER. This also has a list of available support services, social services, death scene clean-up services.

OTHER MEDICAL EXAMINER. Grief groups.

MEDICAL EXAMINER. A funeral director he or she works with the AI/NoK in the case of –

OTHER MEDICAL EXAMINER. Authorized Individual slash Next of Kin.

MEDICAL EXAMINER. Jill.

OTHER MEDICAL EXAMINER. Okay.

MEDICAL EXAMINER. We talked about this.

OTHER MEDICAL EXAMINER. Okay.

MEDICAL EXAMINER. Because it just makes it impossible –

> **OTHER MEDICAL EXAMINER** *looks at her nails.*

Your funeral director will help you as the AI –

As the authorized individual to complete the registration of death form. You'll need Mr. Martin's full name, address, DOB, DOD, the name of his parents, his soc, his occupation and his marital status. Then he or she can get in touch with us and we can release the body.

CURTIS. Okay.

MEDICAL EXAMINER. Okay. Okay well then.

CURTIS. Thank you.

OTHER MEDICAL EXAMINER. He was young.

> **CURTIS** *nods.*

He sure read a lot of books.

MEDICAL EXAMINER. Okay.

OTHER MEDICAL EXAMINER. Okay.

> *They wheel the gurney out of the apartment.*
> **CURTIS** *stands and looks around the*
> *apartment. Exits. The sound of wind.*

8.

At the funeral parlor. A **MORTICIAN** *wheels*
NATE *into the prep room. The* **MORTICIAN** *and*
her **ASSISTANT** *wash* **NATE***'s body.*

ASSISTANT. I had to bail my sister Valerie out of jail yesterday. In Queens.

MORTICIAN. What'd she do?

ASSISTANT. She'd punched a meter maid guy.

MORTICIAN. Oh boy.

ASSISTANT. Because he gave her a parking ticket. When I got down there she was like "I've never gotten a ticket. For anything. Not for speeding. Not even for an illegal turn, or going through a red light, not for anything, ever, never!" And she was "My record was spotless! But that goddamn meter maid guy didn't even care! He wouldn't even listen to me. He coulda let me off with a warning!" I was like "Valerie."

MORTICIAN. Oh boy.

ASSISTANT. They impounded her car.

MORTICIAN. Mm-mm.

ASSISTANT. According to her, her rights have been violated. But I dunno. When I was down there, I saw this guy I knew from high school, he's a rookie cop and I waved at him, and he was about to come over and say hi to me but then he saw Valerie and backed up and left the room. Valerie told me "That rookie cop friend of yours is a prick." When I was driving her home. She said he pretended not to know her when they brought her in, even though she yelled at him "You know my sister, mister, my sister Allison, I know you know her. You bastard prick."

MORTICIAN. I'm not sure you're allowed to call the police "bastards."

ASSISTANT. I don't think you are, either.

MORTICIAN. I'm pretty sure.

They work in silence for a moment.

MORTICIAN. Your sister's a little crazy.

ASSISTANT. She showed up last night at my apartment at two-thirty in the morning. I buzzed her up but I was like "What are you doing here, Valerie? It's late." She was wearing all black. She had three cans of spray paint.

MORTICIAN. What was she going to spray paint?

ASSISTANT. That meter maid guy's car. The guy who gave her the ticket.

MORTICIAN. Oh no.

ASSISTANT. Uh-huh. She said she found his address and she was going over there.

MORTICIAN. Oh boy.

ASSISTANT. I was like "No you're not." She was "Yes we are." I was like "We are? We are? No we are not, Valerie."

MORTICIAN. Oh boy.

ASSISTANT. She was like "You're not going to help me? That guy was an asshole!"

MORTICIAN. Did you tell her no?

ASSISTANT. Yeah. But she was "I always help you." I said "I know you do, but," and she was "Always! Whenever you need help, I help you." I said "I bailed you out!" She said "You're a snake, I can see that now, that's becoming obvious this very minute, I need a hand, I've been hurt, I've been wronged and you're going to stand by and allow it to happen to me without lifting a finger!"

MORTICIAN. Shut the front door.

ASSISTANT. She kept screaming at me "You're a snake! You're a snake!"

MORTICIAN. Shut the front door!

ASSISTANT. I did. I pushed her out of my apartment and shut the door on her.

MORTICIAN. Good!

ASSISTANT. I don't know. This morning I found "snake" exclamation exclamation exclamation point spray painted on the sidewalk outside my building.

MORTICIAN. Your sister's crazy. Look in the bucket for a nude lipstick.

ASSISTANT. How about this one?

MORTICIAN. That'll do. When we're done with Mr. Martin here, I want you to run to T.J. Maxx and get a bra for Mrs. Langford. Her family forgot to send one with her clothes.

ASSISTANT. Okay.

People are crazy. Especially in my family.

MORTICIAN. Oh boy.

ASSISTANT. My sister's always been a perfectionist. I think that ticket kinda I think it was just too much for her.

How's Brandon?

MORTICIAN. He's good. He likes his botany class. He told me there's a plant that lives in the jungle, way up in the trees, it hangs there, it doesn't have any roots, it sits on a tree branch, it's called a bromeliad, bormelad, bromeiladle, and its leaves are like a waxy cup and the cup catches water and a frog lives in the water, like a little tree frog, and then! Then! You're never going to believe this one, then! A fly lands on the plant's leaf and, because it's waxy, the bug slides down and drowns in the water and the frog eats it and the frog's poop is what the plant lives on!

ASSISTANT. Huh.

MORTICIAN. He loves botany.

 A buzzer.

I'll leave this here.

ASSISTANT. Okay.

MORTICIAN. Don't forget the eye caps.

ASSISTANT. I won't.

 The **MORTICIAN** *exits.*

9.

The **MORTICIAN** *is rubbing her hands.* **CURTIS**
*hands her a suit, a shirt, underwear, socks, a
handkerchief, and a pair of shoes.*

MORTICIAN. Hi hello good afternoon.

CURTIS. Hi, I brought these for Nate. For Mr. Martin.

MORTICIAN. Oh good.

CURTIS. I want you to tie the tie in a Windsor knot. That's
how he always tied his ties. And fold this and put it in
his breast pocket.

MORTICIAN. Okay.

CURTIS. I shined his shoes.

MORTICIAN. Okay.

> **CURTIS** *hands her some cufflinks.*

CURTIS. And will you use these cufflinks. They're mine, but
I'd like him to have them.

MORTICIAN. These are beautiful.

CURTIS. He always liked them.

MORTICIAN. Okay.

CURTIS. I think that's everything.

MORTICIAN. I have one more thing for you to sign.

CURTIS. Okay.

MORTICIAN. Have you got a minute?

CURTIS. Sure.

MORTICIAN. Come with me into the office and we'll finish up.

CURTIS. Okay.

> *In the prep room the* **ASSISTANT** *changes the
> radio station and a pop song comes on. She
> does a small dance as she works on* **NATE**'s
> *body.*
>
> *The* **MORTICIAN** *enters. Changes the radio
> station back to classical music. She and the*

      ASSISTANT *dress* **NATE***'s body in the clothes that* **CURTIS** *has given her.*

MORTICIAN. We set?

ASSISTANT. Yup.

MORTICIAN. Okay. Let's get him dressed.

10.

At the service. **CURTIS** *is giving a eulogy.* **NATE'S SISTER,** *the* **MORTICIAN,** *and the* **ASSISTANT** *stand to the side.*

CURTIS. A teacher asked her students "What does your father do?" And little Susie says "My father is a car mechanic." And little Justin says "My father is a doctor." And little Heather says "My father is a tax accountant." And little Ricky says "My father is dead." And the teacher asks little Ricky "What did your father do before he died?" and little Ricky says "Aggggh!"

> **CURTIS** *laughs. No one else does.* **CURTIS** *smiles a bit, sad, and looks away.*
>
> *Then:*

I am very sad about Nate. I –

And I wish –

I um –

> *He can't speak anymore.*

NATE'S SISTER. *(Puts her arm around* **CURTIS'** *shoulders.)* My brother would be so happy that you all came. To say good-bye to him. I am so happy to know that he had so many loving friends.

I didn't see Nate as often as I would have liked to. He didn't love Milwaukee. But I was happy knowing he was so happy in New York, and knowing he was always surrounded by so many things that he did love. The theater and museums and art and the bright lights of the big city and the noise and everything.

I worried every now and then that he must be lonely here all alone but now I see I shouldn't have worried.

I remember he came home to us once and he explained to us that he liked being able to just walk out onto the street and be surrounded by people. And he liked that. Walking among people. And he said the oddest thing to me once, he said: "Sometimes it's easier to be kind to people if you don't know them." I know that was important to him. To be kind. So maybe that's why he stayed here. And didn't want to come home.

And I guess you could be lonely anywhere. Even Milwaukee sometimes is. But. No. Um. I.

Um.

I really just want to thank all of you for coming.

> **NATE'S SISTER** *and* **CURTIS** *exit. The* **ASSISTANT** *and the* **MORTICIAN** *exit.*

11.

In a blackout:

NATE VOICEOVER. I hear footsteps on earth. I hear a car door open and then shut. I hear an engine turn over. Wheels moving on gravel. A car pulling away.

And other car doors opening and the murmur of people making decisions. And then more car doors closing with –

And starting up and pulling away.

Now chairs being folded up and stacked on the back of a truck and young men laughing.

One is telling a joke about something that happened last night I think.

Now I hear the rumble of the backhoe and a mountain of dirt thudding down.

And something else. I don't know what it is.

And voices made soft by the earth.

And then the truck goes.

A silence.

And then very faintly, I hear a whisper of wind through trees, a flap of wings, the cawing of a crow. I can hear distant houses settling into themselves and the hum of cars on a far-off road the hum of hum of of and the murmur of and the and the thick sounds of –

And I feel the weight of the earth pressing down on the wood of my casket and and –

and water dripping through soil and past stone –

and water –

and past stone.

12.

Lights up. **NATE** *stands and speaks, his own voice.*

NATE. I have so much to tell you.

I woke up, startled because something I dreamed was going to come true.

I wanted to sit down but someone was in my chair. I saw a bird fly away. I had a thought of my mother, of a road and black trees and snow.

"Hello little monkey. One two three four. Hello monkey."

Suddenly melancholy:

Our house was pulled down to build another one.

But then reminding himself:

Everything is good. Everything is a poem.

Oh and –

There is a blinding light. Then darkness. Lights slowly up onstage. It's empty.

End of Play